LOST KITTIES

SQUAD GOALS
#NOMZ

written by
Maggie Fischer

studio fun
INTERNATIONAL

PRE-LEVEL 1: ASPIRING READERS

 LEVEL 1: EARLY READERS

 LEVEL 2: DEVELOPING READERS

 LEVEL 3: ENGAGED READERS

- Repetition of longer sentence patterns with variation of placement of subjects, verbs, and adjectives
- Most of the vocabulary should be familiar to first graders
- Introduction of more complex spelling patterns and letter-sound relationships

 LEVEL 4: FLUENT READERS

studio fun
INTERNATIONAL

Studio Fun International
An imprint of Printers Row Publishing Group
A division of Readerlink Distribution Services, LLC
10350 Barnes Canyon Road, Suite 100, San Diego, CA 92121
www.studiofun.com

Written by Maggie Fischer
Illustrated by Hasbro and Wilson Tortosa &
Michael Bartolo of Glass House Graphics
Designed by Kara Kenna

Library of Congress Cataloging-in-Publication Data is available upon request.

Printers Row Publishing Group is a division of Readerlink Distribution Services, LLC.
Studio Fun International is a registered trademark of Readerlink Distribution Services, LLC.
All notations of errors or omissions should be addressed to Studio Fun International,
Editorial Department, at the above address.

ISBN: 978-0-7944-4430-3

Manufactured, printed, and assembled in Shenzhen, China. First printing, January 2019. RRD/01/19

23 22 21 20 19 1 2 3 4 5

Licensed by:

Chomp goes to the grocery store to buy the **FIRE FUR** peppers. She also buys a carton of milk to drink—shopping for peppers is thirsty work!

When Chomp gets home, she makes a big bowl of hot sauce. Chomp chops up the **FIRE FUR** peppers and adds them to the bowl.

Chomp sniffs the sauce. **SPICY**—just the way Chomp likes it. She looks around for a bottle to put her hot sauce in.

Chomp spots the now-empty milk carton that she bought at the store. Chomp pours her hot sauce into the milk carton.

Chomp goes to wash her paws before eating. When she leaves, a curious Sketch peeks into the kitchen. Sketch sees the milk carton on the counter and her whiskers twitch.

Sketch **LOVES** milk. She loves it more than catnaps! Sketch grabs the milk carton off of the counter and runs!

Chomp comes back to the kitchen and gasps. Her hot sauce is **GONE!** Chomp's tummy grumbles.

"Don't worry, tummy," Chomp says. "I'll find my sauce!"

Chomp starts to search when she stumbles across a howling Sketch! There's an empty milk carton beside her, her blue fur has turned **RED**, and smoke is coming from her ears.

"Oh no!" Chomp cries. "Sketch drank my hot sauce thinking it was milk!"

Chomp runs to the kitchen and gives Sketch some real milk to wash down the hot sauce.

Gasping, Sketch's fur fades back to blue.

"Sorry, Chomp. I didn't mean to steal your hot sauce!" Sketch says. Chomp hands Sketch a taco.

The hot sauce is just right in small bites.

PURR-FECT!

STUFFS'S SUPER-SECRET SNACK

STUFFS ONLY LIKES THE BEST OF EVERYTHING.

He wears the **FANCIEST** clothes, goes to the **FANCIEST** restaurants, and eats the **FANCIEST** foods. He has to—he's a food critic! If Stuffs writes a good review of the food, restaurants will get lots of kitty customers!

Stuffs tells kitties his favorite food is caviar—
fish eggs. It's very **FANCY**, just like Stuffs! But
Stuffs favorite food is actually **FRENCH FRIES**!

Stuffs used to turn up his whiskers at fast
food. But one night, Stuffs was very hungry.
And even though Stuffs loves fancy food, this
kitty cannot cook.

Stuffs's tummy was groaning, and moaning, and grumbling! Then, a **WONDERFUL** smell hit his nose. Sniffing, Stuffs followed that amazing smell all the way to a fast-food restaurant.

Hungry Stuffs walked in without thinking. When he saw them making French fries, his stomach roared!

Stuffs ordered twelve extra-large cartons of fries and ate every single one.

Ever since that night, Stuffs hasn't been able to get French fries out of his head. He's started dreaming about them! So Stuffs hatched a super-secret plan.

He went back to the fast-food restaurant and made a deal: Stuffs would come to the restaurant every night and buy fries. If they didn't tell anyone that Stuffs liked French fries, he would pay **EXTRA**!

For months, Stuffs's plan worked **PURR-FECTLY**! By day, he was a fancy food critic. By night, he secretly snacked to his heart's content.

Everything was going great, until Stuffs got **the note**.

Slipped under his door, the note said:

I KNOWZ WHERE U GO IN THE NIGHTTIME

On the back was a photo of Stuffs, munching on fries.

Oh no! Some kitty found out about Stuffs's super-secret snacking!

Picking up the note again, Stuffs spots another small line written on the note.

MEET ME AT DA PLACE 4 FRIEZ. COME ALONE.

He hides in some bushes near the front entrance. Stuffs gasps as he sees Cheesy walk up!

"Cheesy? You're the one sending me scary notes?" Stuffs asks.

"Scary?" Cheesy repeats, looking confused. "I just saw that you got a deal on fries! And you know what goes well with French fries? PIZZA!" Cheesy starts to drool at the thought of pizza.

"You mean; you don't want to tell every kitty in town that I secretly love fast food?" Stuffs asks.

"No! I just want to eat fries with you" Cheesy says.

3 CHAMPION CHUNKS

THUNK

"OH, MAN! I MISSED AGAIN!"

Chunks groans. She's been practicing for the Grand Hairball Hacking Competition for hours now, and she's still missing the target. The point of the competition is to cough up a glorious hairball that sails through the air and lands in the contestant's cup.

Chunks loves anything **GROSS**, so this competition is purr-fect for her! But she keeps missing the cup! Maybe a lunch break will clear her head.

Chunks piles rotting tuna on pickled onions, takes a big bite, and starts to chew. **STINKY** breath is the best!

After lunch, she walks by Thimble's room and sees him working on his obstacle course. Maybe he could help her with her hairball toss!

In Thimble's room, Chunks trips over some of the yarn he has hanging by the door.

Thimble just keeps weaving through the yarn set up all over his room.

Chunks watches him . . . maybe being more flexible will help her aim? But Chunks keeps ending up tangled in yarn.

Finally, she does it right, just like Thimble! Excited, Chunks thanks him as she rushes back to her target practice!

Squinting at the cup on the floor, Chunks starts to cough. Out comes a hairball, heading straight for the cup! Almost . . . almost . . . no! She **MISSED**!

Chunks decides she needs more practice. But her green fur is out of hairballs! Chunks decides she needs a fur loan.

Stopping by the bathroom, she sees Drizzle taking his fourteenth bath of the day.

"Drizzle! Can you do me a favor? Pretty please with pickled onions on top?" Chunks asks.

What iz it, Chunks?

"Can you lend me some of your fur to lick? I need more hairballs to practice with for the Grand Hairball Hacking Competition," Chunks explains. Drizzle shudders.

"And get your germs on me? **NO WAY!** I have to take another bath just thinking about it!" Drizzle cries.

Discouraged, Chunks heads back to her room. Flufferton is waiting for her.

"I heard you need extra fur," Flufferton says, pointing at her fluffy coat. "I *always* have extra fur."

Excited, Chunks licks Flufferton's fur and makes a giant hairball. She tosses the hairball with all of her might, and **BAM**!

It's a **SLAM CHUNK**!

LOAFY'S SMOKY TOAST

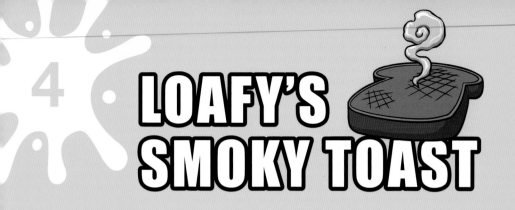

LOAFY GLANCES AT THE SMOKE POURING OUT OF THE TOASTER AND SIGHS.

Pulling blackened bread out of the toaster, he takes a bite. Just as he suspected—burnt again! Loafy keeps chewing, his face falling. Lately his toaster has been getting too excited. His bread has started coming out less "LIGHTLY TOASTED" and more "FIRE ROASTED."

Loafy has tried plugging the toaster into a different socket. He's tried plugging it into the *same* socket. He even unplugged it altogether. That test had the worst results.

The sound of a skateboard comes from the hall as Scoops squeezes his cone past the doorway.

"Scoops, can *you* fix my toaster?" Loafy asks.

"No can do, my bread-loving buddy," Scoops tells him. "My paws and wires do *not* mix."

Loafy looks miserably at his BURNT toast.

"Hey, cheer up! I know who can help," Scoops says. Loafy's face brightens.

"Who?" Loafy asks.

"Professor Purrkins can fix anything!" Scoops replies. Loafy races off to the professor's lab!

"Professor Purrkins, can you fix my toaster?"
Loafy asks.

I will try wiff all my brainz.

Professor Purrkins inspects the toaster and starts to laugh.

"What's so funny? Do you know what's wrong?"
Loafy asks.

"Loafy, the dial was turned all the way up!" The professor shows Loafy the dial: turned past "TOAST, TOASTIER, TOASTIEST," and set to "EXTRA CRISPY."

Loafy turns the dial back down, smiling.

MEOW WOW, Professor! U saved my toast!

"Maybe you could spare a piece?" the professor asks.

Loafy nods, laughing. Who knew that appliance repair could be so DELICIOUS?

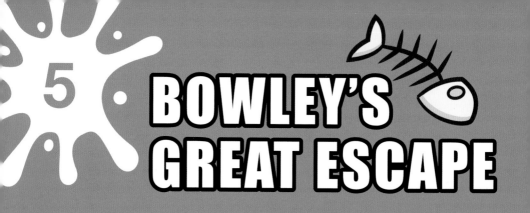

5 BOWLEY'S GREAT ESCAPE

TODAY IS THE DAY. THE GREATEST OF ALL DAYS.

The day that all of the other kitties will be talking about until the end of time. Today, Bowley gets out.

Bowley should clarify: he can already get out of his bowl. The top is open, so he just hops on out! It's when he leaves the house that things start to get FISHY.

See, Bowley loves seafood. Crab, lobster, tuna, salmon, shrimp—he loves it all! He even keeps goldfish in his bowl for an easy snack. But his love of fish can get him into trouble.

The last time Bowley left the house, he broke into the Meow-terey Aquarium. He ended up in a big tank, trying to eat a dolphin. It took five aquarium employees to get him out of there!

Now Bowley's in his bowl, and he is no longer allowed at that aquarium. **EVER**. Talk about a flea in your fur!

But Bowley heard that a new seafood restaurant just opened up nearby. If he escapes, it'll be a **FISHY BUFFET**! But the kitties *know* that Bowley gets a little fur crazy over fish. So Noperz is in charge of keeping him inside for the day.

Noperz walks into the room, scowling. Opening the cabinet, he grabs a bag of kibble.

"**YUCK**! How can you eat that stuff?" Bowley asks, snatching a goldfish out of his bowl and swallowing with a noisy gulp. Noperz just glares.

If you let me out of here, I could get you real food!" Bowley says. "Crabs the size of footballs! Schools of fish!"

Noperz just chews his kibble. Bowley sighs. This was going to be harder than he thought!

Bowley tries bribing Noperz next, but he doesn't like *anything*! Bowley's laser pointer? Not interested. Bowley's catnip? Not a chance! Bowley's bouncy ball? He batted it off the counter. RUDE!

Bowley decides to put his escape mission on hold and watch TV. He turns on a show about the ocean.

Feeling the couch dip, Bowley turns to see Noperz sitting next to him.

"I like whales," Noperz says quietly.

"Me too," Bowley replies, starting to grin. "They look **DELICIOUS**."

Noperz laughs, shaking his head.

U know what, Noperz? U iz not so bad.

NOPE.

TABLE of CONTENTS

1 CHOMP'S CHILI PEPPER

CHOMP IS IN THE MOOD TO EAT SOMETHING TASTY.

Tacos are her favorite treat! But her super-spicy hot sauce still isn't hot enough. It needs something special.

Chomp decides to get the hottest pepper in the world: the **FIRE FUR**. With the help of the **FIRE FUR** peppers, Chomp knows that her hot sauce will be *purr-fect*!